Happy Easter Tad 2004

I Love you Little Buddy with all my Heart ♡

Ninny Bug

Goodnight, Baby Monster

by Laura Leuck
illustrated by Nigel McMullen

HarperCollins*Publishers*

Goodnight, baby monster,
all warm in your den.

Goodnight, baby goblin,
it's bedtime again.

Goodnight, baby mummy,
wrapped up in your tomb.

Goodnight, baby witch,
asleep near your broom.

Goodnight, baby bat,
as you hang from your eave.

Goodnight, baby spider,
so safe in your weave.

Goodnight, baby dragon,
curled up in your bed.

Goodnight, baby ghost,
your story's been read.

Goodnight, baby swamp-thing,
all snuggled in slime.

Goodnight, baby owl,
it's lullaby time.

Goodnight, baby black cat,
no prancing or prowling.

Goodnight, baby werewolf,
no growling or howling.

Goodnight, baby vulture,
tucked up in your nest.

Goodnight, baby gremlin,
it's time now to rest.

Goodnight, spooky babies,
now don't peep or creep.

It's time for *all* babies
to fall fast asleep!

To my grandparents Grace and William Youngworth
—L.L.

To Mum and Lindsey
—N.M.

Goodnight, Baby Monster
Text copyright © 2002 by Laura Leuck
Illustrations copyright © 2002 by Nigel McMullen
Printed in Hong Kong. All rights reserved.
www.harperchildrens.com

Library of Congress Cataloging-in-Publication Data
Leuck, Laura.
Goodnight, baby monster / by Laura Leuck ;
illustrated by Nigel McMullen.
p.   cm.
Summary: A bedtime rhyme for baby monsters and other spooky creatures
ISBN 0-06-029151-6 — ISBN 0-06-029152-4 (lib. bdg.)
[1. Bedtime—Fiction.   2. Monsters—Fiction.
3. Stories in rhyme.]   I. McMullen, Nigel, ill.   II. Title.
PZ8.3.L565 Go   2002   2001016849   [E]—dc21

Designed by Stephanie Bart-Horvath
1 2 3 4 5 6 7 8 9 10
❖
First Edition